A Pie Went By

by Carolyn Dunn

illustrated by Christopher Santoro

HARPERCOLLINS*PUBLISHERS*

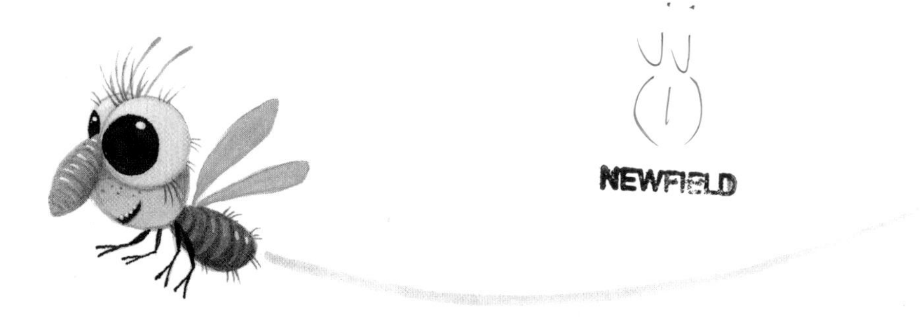

To Max, Michael, and Ruby Jo—with love from Gramma.
Special thanks to Sarah T.

—C.D.

For my very own Queen Bea

—C.S.

The art for this book was created with watercolor and gouache.

 http://www.harperchildrens.com

Library of Congress Cataloging-in-Publication Data
Dunn, Carolyn (Carolyn B.)
A pie went by / by Carolyn Dunn ; illustrated by Christopher Santoro.
p. cm.
SUMMARY: King Bing plans to offer a pie to Queen Bea when he asks her to marry him, but the animals he passes on the way have other ideas.
ISBN 0-06-028807-8. — ISBN 0-06-028808-6 (lib. bdg.)
[1. Kings, queens, rulers, etc.—Fiction. 2. Animals—Fiction. 3. Pies—Fiction.] I. Santoro, Christopher, ill. II. Title.
PZ7.D92152 Pi 1999 98-16790
[E]—dc21 CIP
AC

Typography by Al Cetta 1 2 3 4 5 6 7 8 9 10 ❖ First Edition

King Bing's Easy Cherry Pie

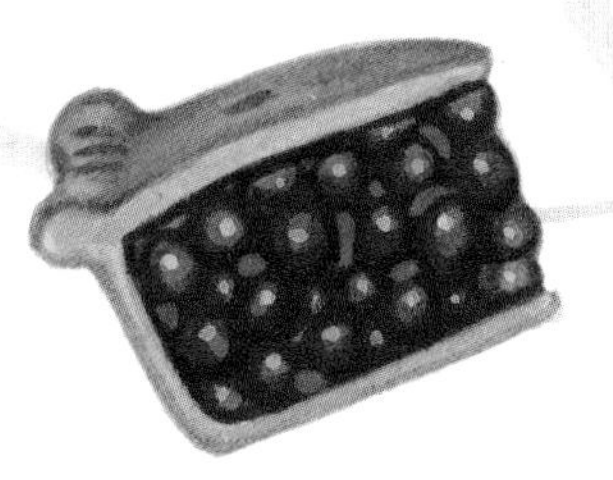

- 1 1/4 cup oats
- 1 cup brown sugar (packed down)
- 3/4 cup flour
- 1/2 teaspoon cinnamon
- 1 1/2 sticks butter or margarine
- 1 20-ounce can cherry pie filling

Always have an adult help you when you're cooking, especially when you're near the stove.

Preheat the oven to 375°.

FOR THE TOPPING:

In a large mixing bowl combine the oats, brown sugar, flour, and cinnamon. Stir. It's okay if there are still brown sugar lumps when you're done stirring. Put the butter or margarine into the mixing bowl and use a table knife to cut it up into small pieces. Then use the knife, a pastry blender, or even your fingers to mix the butter or margarine into the dry ingredients. When you're done, the mixture should look like bread crumbs.

FOR THE FILLING:

Grease a 10" pie pan and empty the cherry pie filling into it.
Spread the topping evenly over the filling.

Bake for 35–40 minutes.

Let the pie cool before you eat it. Queen Bea likes this pie even better with vanilla ice cream on top.

One fine day good King Bing walked along the path to the castle, carrying a pie on his head. “How absurd,” said a passing bird. “A pie went by!”

In the meadow near the path grazed the castle cow.

"Where are you going, King Bing?" she asked.

"Ah, my dear friend," said the king. "I'm taking this pie to Queen Bea. I'm going to ask her to marry me."

The cow eyed the pie. It looked very good.

"Bow now," said the cow.

"Sorry, no time," said King Bing, hurrying off down the path with the cow right behind him.

"Highbrow," mooed the cow.

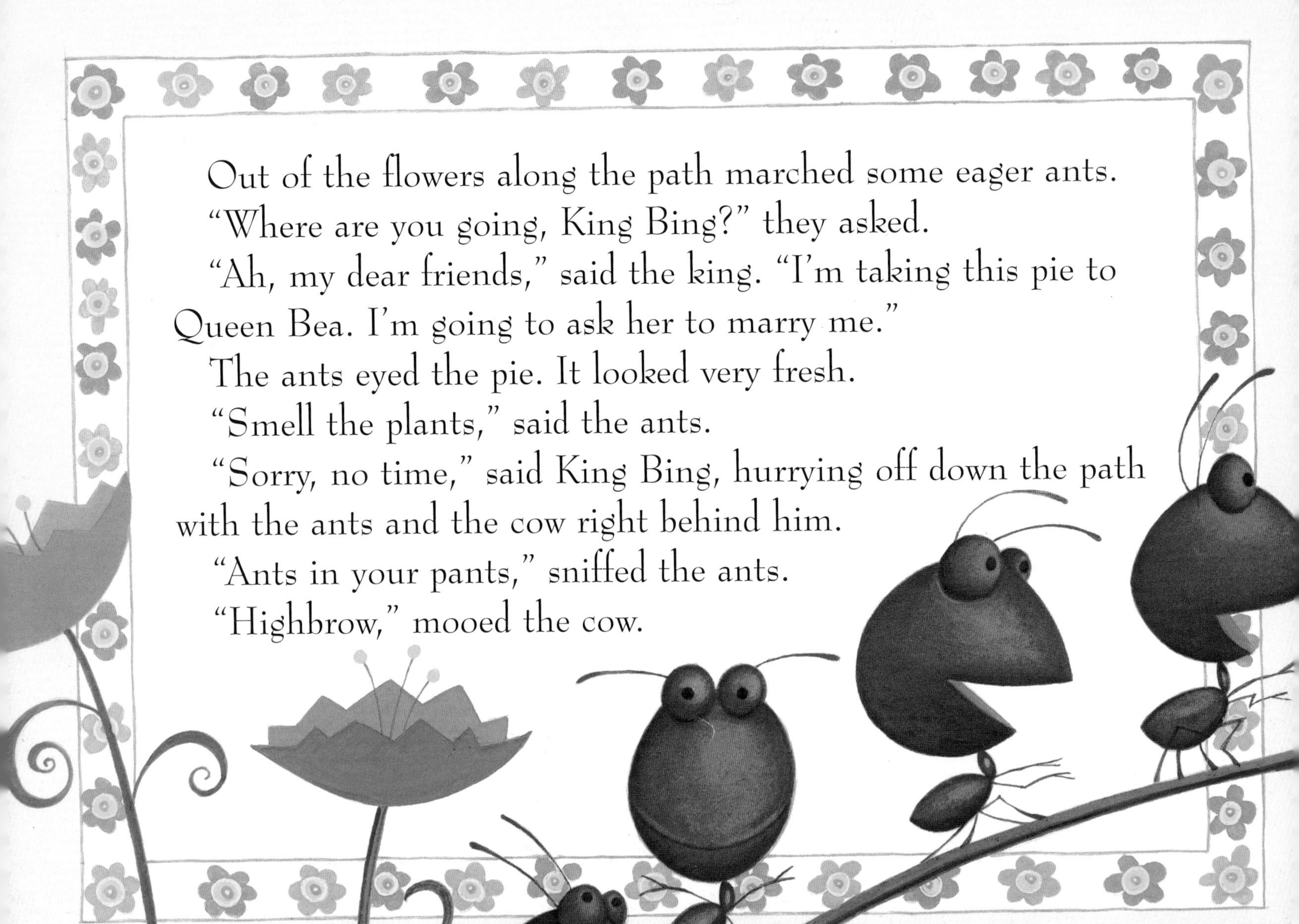

Out of the flowers along the path marched some eager ants.

"Where are you going, King Bing?" they asked.

"Ah, my dear friends," said the king. "I'm taking this pie to Queen Bea. I'm going to ask her to marry me."

The ants eyed the pie. It looked very fresh.

"Smell the plants," said the ants.

"Sorry, no time," said King Bing, hurrying off down the path with the ants and the cow right behind him.

"Ants in your pants," sniffed the ants.

"Highbrow," mooed the cow.

From the drawbridge over the moat watched the dungeon dog.

"Where are you going, King Bing?" he asked.

"Ah, my dear friend," said the king. "I'm taking this pie to Queen Bea. I'm going to ask her to marry me."

The dog eyed the pie. It looked very tasty.

"Play leapfrog?" asked the dog.

"Sorry, no time," said King Bing, hurrying over the drawbridge with the dog and the ants and the cow right behind him.

"What a hog," growled the dog.

"Ants in your pants," sniffed the ants.

"Highbrow," mooed the cow.

In the courtyard beside the castle pecked the cheerful chick.

"Where are you going, King Bing?" she asked.

"Ah, my dear friend," said the king. "I'm taking this pie to Queen Bea. I'm going to ask her to marry me."

The chick eyed the pie. It looked very sweet.

"Pick up a stick," said the chick.

"Sorry, no time," said King Bing, hurrying into the castle with the chick and the dog and the ants and the cow right behind him.

"Dirty trick," chirped the chick.

"What a hog," growled the dog.

"Ants in your pants," sniffed the ants.

"Highbrow," mooed the cow.

Meanwhile, around the pie buzzed a fearless fly.

"Where are you going, King Bing?" he asked.

"Ah, my dear friend," said the king. "I'm taking this pie to Queen Bea. I'm going to ask her to marry me."

The fly eyed the pie. It looked delicious!

"Your shoe's untied," said the fly.

"Sorry, no time," said King Bing, hurrying toward the throne room with the fly and the chick and the dog and the ants and the cow right behind him.

"Wise guy," buzzed the fly.

"Dirty trick," chirped the chick.

"What a hog," growled the dog.

"Ants in your pants," sniffed the ants.

"Highbrow," mooed the cow.

At last King Bing reached the throne and knelt before the queen. "Dear Queen Bea," he said. "Will you marry me?"

"No," said the queen.

"No?" said the king.

"No?" said the cow.

"No?" said the ants.

"No?" said the dog.

"No?" said the chick.

"But why?" asked the fly.

“Why should I?” answered the queen. “What’s so special about the king that would make me want to become Queen Bea Bing?”

“Ummmm . . .” said the king. He looked over at his friends.

“Nice eyebrows,” said the cow.

“He can dance,” said the ants.

“He’s learning to jog,” said the dog.

“He’s quite lovesick,” said the chick.

“Try the pie,” said the fly.

Queen Bea eyed the pie. She stuck in her finger and took a taste. She smacked her lips. "Just kidding," she said. "I'll marry you, King Bing."

"Oh wow," mooed the cow.

"True romance," sniffed the ants.

"Pour the grog," growled the dog.

"Kiss her quick," chirped the chick.

"What about the pie?" buzzed the fly.

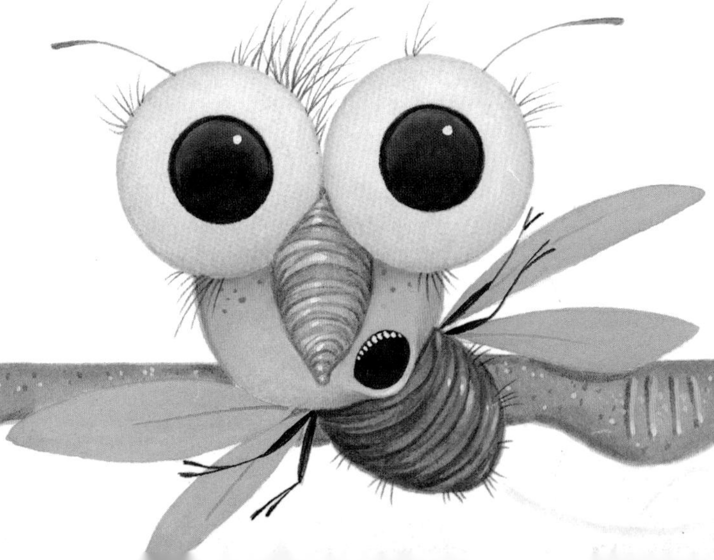

“Ah, my dear friends,” said the king. “How can I ever thank you for helping me in my hour of need?” He bowed his most gallant bow. The pie slowly slid off his head and splattered all over the floor.

“What now?” mooed the cow.
“Unlucky chance,” sniffed the ants.
“Fell like a log,” growled the dog.
“Makes me sick,” chirped the chick.

"Never cry over spilled pie," buzzed the fly. "Dig in!"

"Silly things," said the king. "Come, my dear Queen Bea. We have a wedding cake to bake. I'll teach you to cook."

"I have a better idea," said Queen Bea. "You cook and I'll eat, and we'll live happily ever after."

And so they did.